$$\varphi(\ell, s)$$

$$F(x+\xi_1)\,d\xi_1 \cdot \varphi(x+\xi_1, \xi_2-\xi_1)\,d\xi_2$$

$$= F(x+\xi_2)\,d\xi_2\,\varphi(x+\xi_2, \xi_1-\xi_2)\,d\xi_1$$

$$(F + \xi_1 F')\left[\varphi(x, \xi_2-\xi_1) + \xi_1 \varphi'(x, \xi_2-\xi_1)\right]$$

$$(F + \xi_2 F')\left[\varphi(x, \xi_1-\xi_2) + \xi_2 \varphi'(x, \xi_1-\xi_2)\right]$$

Spezialfall $\xi_2 = 0$

$$(F + \xi_1 F')\left[\varphi(x, -\xi_1) + \xi_1 \varphi'(x, -\xi_1)\right] = F\,\varphi(x, \xi_1)$$

$$F\{\varphi(x, -\xi) - \varphi(x, \xi)\} + \xi_x\{F'\varphi(x, -\xi) + F\varphi'(x, -\xi)\} = 0$$

$$F\{\varphi(x, \xi) - \varphi(x, -\xi)\} - \xi\{F'\varphi(x, \xi) + F\varphi'(x, \xi)\} = 0$$

$$\frac{\partial}{\partial x}\underbrace{\{F(\varphi(x, \xi) - \varphi(x, -\xi))\}}_{\psi(x, \xi)} = 0$$

$$F \cdot \psi(x, \xi) = \text{konst.} \chi(\xi)$$

$$\int_0^\infty \varphi(x, -\xi)\,d\xi = -\int_0^{-\infty}\varphi(x, \xi)\,d\xi = \int_{-\infty}^0 \varphi(x, \xi)\,d\xi$$

$$\int_{-\infty}^{+\infty}\xi\,\varphi(x, -\xi)\,d\xi$$
$$= -\int_{-\infty}^{+\infty}$$

$$\longrightarrow -2F\overline{\xi} + \frac{\partial}{\partial x}\left\{F\int_{-\infty}^{\infty}\xi^2\,\varphi(x, -\xi)\,d\xi\right\} = 0$$

$$-2\cdot F\,\overline{\xi} + \frac{\partial}{\partial x}\left\{F\,\overline{\xi^2}\right\} = 0$$

For Claire & Chloe –J.T.

For my parents –W.E.

——— GLOSSARY ———

BÜRGERMEISTER (BUR-ge-MICE-ter): the German word for "mayor."

GESUNDHEIT (ge-ZUND-hite): the German word for "health." It's what people in German-speaking countries say after someone sneezes. Many English-speaking countries have borrowed this tradition.

MAUSI (MOW-zi): German for "little mouse." Often used as an endearing nickname for a young child.

MEIN SPATZI (mine SHPAT-zi): German for "my little sparrow." Another term of endearment.

SCHNITZEL (SHNIT-sel): a popular food in Germany and Austria made from a thin cutlet of meat usually coated with egg and bread crumbs and then fried.

Text copyright © 2014 by Jacqueline Tourville
Jacket art and interior illustrations copyright © 2014 by Wynne Evans

Grateful acknowledgment is made to the Hebrew University of Jerusalem and the Princeton University Press for permission to reprint images from Albert Einstein's "Zürich Notebook," copyright © 1987 the Hebrew University of Jerusalem. Reprinted by permission of Princeton University Press.

Visit us on the Web! randomhouse.com/kids
Educators and librarians, for a variety of teaching tools, visit us at RHTeachersLibrarians.com

Library of Congress Cataloging-in-Publication Data
Tourville, Jacqueline.
Albie's first word : A tale inspired by Albert Einstein's childhood / Jacqueline Tourville ; jacket art and interior illustrations [Wynne Evans].—First edition.
pages cm
Summary: Because three-year-old Albie, who would one day be known as Albert Einstein, has never spoken his concerned family takes him to a doctor who recommends a series of activities that might stimulate him to talk.
ISBN 978-0-307-97893-6 (trade) — ISBN 978-0-307-97894-3 (glb) — ISBN 978-0-307-97895-0 (ebook)
1. Einstein, Albert, 1879–1955—Childhood and youth—Juvenile fiction. [1. Einstein, Albert, 1879–1955—Childhood and youth—Fiction. 2. Speech—Fiction.] I. Evans, Wynne, illustrator. II. Title.
PZ7.T6477Alb 2014 [E]—dc23 2013007891

The text of this book is set in Aged.
The illustrations were rendered in oil glaze and finished digitally.

MANUFACTURED IN CHINA
2 4 6 8 10 9 7 5 3 1
First Edition

Albie's First Word

A TALE INSPIRED BY ALBERT EINSTEIN'S CHILDHOOD

WRITTEN BY Jacqueline Tourville
& ILLUSTRATED BY Wynne Evans

schwartz & wade books · new york

Albie, as everyone called Albert, liked
to do all the things other children did.

He jumped in puddles
after a spring rain,

waded in the blue waters
of the Danube in summer,

collected acorns in autumn,

and in wintertime went ice-skating with his mother,
father, and little sister, Maya.

But there was one thing Albie did not do.

He did not speak. He would not speak. Not one word.

Maya, on the other hand, could say words like "schnitzel" and "gesundheit" by the time she turned one. New words spilled from her mouth like an endless spool of ribbon. She talked to the cat and the cat answered back.

But when Maya spoke to her brother, he never paid much attention.
Albie always seemed busy thinking about something else.

One day, Albie's father gave him a mariner's compass, and before his family's eyes, Albie took it apart and put it back together again. Another time, Albie built a house of cards so high that it looked just like one of Munich's towering cathedrals. When his parents asked in amazement, "How did you do that?" he only smiled.

His worried mother brought him to Dr. Hoffmann, but when the doctor checked Albie's eyes, ears, and throat and tapped on his knee, he couldn't find anything the matter.

"I have seen a few cases like this before, Frau Einstein," the doctor consoled her. "To help the boy talk, you must take him to new places and get him to ask questions."

Dr. Hoffmann's eyes skimmed the calendar on his wall. "Ah, yes!
The orchestra is performing Mozart's *Jupiter* Symphony tonight.
Why not go and see what happens?"

So Albie's family went to the symphony. Albie danced in his seat; he hummed; he stamped his feet to the beat; he even waved his arms just like the conductor.

As soon as the music ended and they rose to leave, his mother asked, "Albie, my darling *mausi*, what did you think?"

Albie spun around in a circle and gave
his mother a hug.

But he didn't say a word.

Albie's father told Dr. Hoffmann what had happened.

"Well, why don't we try this? Take Albie to the university to hear the great Professor Max. His voice is clear and loud, and he is fascinating. That should help," the doctor said.

So the very next day, Albie and his father went to hear Professor Max's astronomy lecture. Sure enough, the professor spoke very slowly and clearly as he described the orbit of the planet Mercury. Albie's father didn't understand a word, but Albie's eyes followed the professor's every movement as he filled the chalkboard with numbers.

When the lecture ended, all the students politely clapped.

Albie jumped up and down.

"What is it, *mein spatzi?* Tell Papa, what makes you so excited?" his father asked.

Albie squeezed his father's hand with happiness.

But he didn't say a word.

Dr. Hoffmann had one last piece of advice. "Being around other children might help. There is a toy boat race in the park tomorrow. Why not go?" The doctor took a model boat from the shelf. "Herr Albie, I present to you my lucky sloop."

Albie's eyes lit up.

So Albie's family went to the park. Albie joined the other children crowded around the boat basin and put Dr. Hoffmann's sloop in the water. A checkered flag waved and the race began!

As the boats sailed across the pond, the children followed.

"Albie wins!" Maya squealed.

Sure enough, the sloop crossed the finish line first, and confetti streamed through the air.

The *bürgermeister* was there to hand out the prizes. Placing a shiny gold trophy in Albie's hands, he said, "It gives me great pleasure to award first prize to . . . Ahhh, excuse me, little boy?" The *bürgermeister* leaned over. "I am sorry, but what is your name?"

Albie looked into the old man's kind eyes,
took a deep breath, and opened his mouth.

His parents clutched each other.

Maya stopped chattering.

The other children

stepped closer.

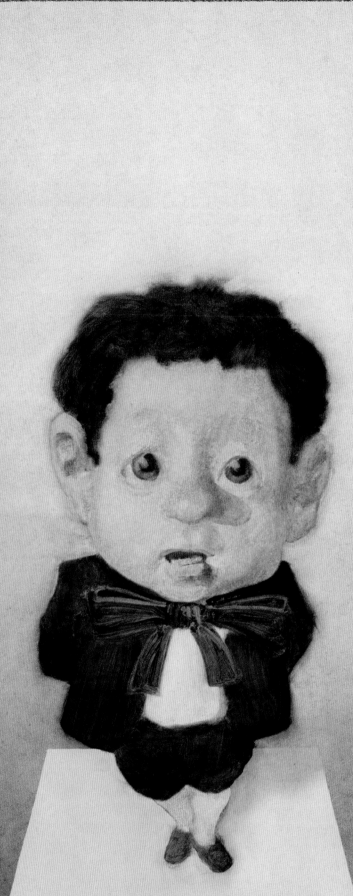

Would Albie say something at last?

After a long moment, Albie smiled shyly.

But he didn't say a word. He simply held
the trophy high over his head in victory.

That night, Albie's parents agreed that if Albie never said so much as a single word in his entire life, they would love him just as he was.

Albie's mother went upstairs to tuck Albie in and say good night.

But when she got there, he wasn't in his bed.

He had pulled a chair to his window and sat gazing at the night sky. Outside, dozens of shooting stars streaked by, their dazzle and shimmer lighting up the darkness.

Albie and his mother stared in silent wonder until his eyes began to droop and he let out a yawn.

But as his mother tucked him in, he suddenly sat up and pointed out the window. And in the sweetest, clearest voice his mother had ever heard, Albie said:

WHY?

Albie would grow up to become Albert Einstein, whose creativity and imagination gave us new ways to solve the mysteries and riddles of the universe. Einstein said, "The important thing is to not stop questioning."

And he never did.

Author's Note

He had such difficulty with language that those around him feared he would never learn.

—Maria "Maja" Einstein

Like most people, I've always known Albert Einstein as the wild-haired genius who revolutionized the world of physics, the freethinker who spoke out for world peace, and the rumpled professor whose eyes twinkled as he stuck his tongue out for the camera.

It was while researching an article on child speech development that I first came across mention of Einstein's late talking. I wondered what his childhood was like, especially the moment the hesitant speaker finally said something!

Einstein was born in 1879 in the German town of Ulm, on the Danube River. Exactly how old he was when he uttered his first words is unknown. However, Einstein would write, "It is true that my parents were worried because I began to speak relatively late, so much so that they contacted a doctor. I can't say how old I was, certainly not less than three."

The future physicist was unusual in other ways, too. Quiet and detached compared to other children, he was a loner who preferred to "engage in daydreaming and meditative musing," according to Philipp Frank, a colleague. Younger sister and lifelong best friend Maja Einstein (pronounced "My-uh"; I have changed the spelling in the story to avoid mispronunciation) recalled her brother's endless fascination with a compass their father gave him, his ease at learning mathematics, and his ability to construct houses of cards fourteen stories tall.

In 1881, the Einstein family moved to Munich. We don't know what remedy the doctor prescribed for Albert's delayed speech or whether his family ever really attended a symphony, heard one of Max Planck's physics lectures, or raced toy boats in Munich's grand Englischer Garten. Einstein's first words, too, have been lost to time.

Einstein published his Special Theory of Relativity in 1905 and his General Theory of Relativity in 1915. In 1921, he won the Nobel Prize in Physics for his work, and his groundbreaking ideas about space and time helped catapult him to worldwide fame. Einstein moved to the United States in 1933 and began teaching at Princeton University. He continued his scientific explorations, became an ardent supporter of nuclear disarmament, and, in his free time, liked to sail and play the violin (Mozart was his favorite).

Einstein once explained in a letter to a friend what fueled his lifelong thirst for knowledge. He credited childhood. "People like you and me never grow old," he wrote. "We never cease to stand like curious children before the great mystery into which we were born."

$$\frac{\partial g_{\varrho\sigma}}{\partial x_\tau} = \sum_{\beta\alpha} g_{\varrho\beta}\,\pi_{\alpha\beta}\,\frac{\partial p_{\alpha\sigma}}{\partial x_\tau} + \sum_{\alpha\beta} g_{\alpha\sigma}\,\pi_{\beta\alpha}\,\frac{\partial p_{\beta\varrho}}{\partial x_\tau}\quad\Big|\ \partial g_{\mu\nu}$$

$$\frac{\partial g_{\mu\nu}}{\partial x_\sigma} = \sum_{\alpha\beta} g_{\mu\alpha}\,p_{\beta\alpha}\,\frac{\partial \pi_{\beta\nu}}{\partial x_\sigma} + \sum_{\alpha\beta} g_{\alpha\nu}\,p_{\beta\alpha}\,\frac{\partial \pi_{\beta\mu}}{\partial x_\sigma}$$

G.

$$\frac{\partial G}{\partial x_\nu} = \sum_{ik}\frac{\partial g_{ik}}{\partial x_\nu} G_{ik} = \sum G\,\frac{\partial g_{ik}}{\partial x_\nu}\gamma_{ik} = -G\sum g_{ik}\frac{\partial \gamma_{ik}}{\partial x_\nu}\quad\text{mll zu letzter Teile}$$

$$\varphi_1 = \sum_{iklm\mu\nu} g_{\mu\nu}\,\frac{\partial \gamma_{ik}}{\partial x_\mu}\frac{\partial g_{lm}}{\partial x_\nu} G_{ik} G_{lm}.\quad\Big|\text{oder}\quad \sum g_{\mu\nu}\,\frac{\partial \gamma_{ik}}{\partial x_\mu}\frac{\partial \gamma_{lm}}{\partial x_\nu}\gamma_{ik}\gamma_{lm}$$

$$\varphi_2 = \sum\frac{1}{\partial x_\mu}\left(\sqrt{G}\,g_{\mu\nu}\,\frac{\partial G^\alpha}{\partial x_\nu}\right)\qquad\qquad \frac{\partial}{\partial x_\mu}\left(\sqrt{G}\,g_{\mu\nu}\,\frac{\partial \psi}{\partial x_\nu}\right)$$

$$= \alpha\sum\frac{\partial}{\partial x_\mu}\left(\sqrt{G}\,g_{\mu\nu}\,G^{\alpha-1}\,\frac{\partial g_{ik}}{\partial x_\nu}G_{ik}\right) \approx \sum\frac{\partial}{\partial x_\mu}\left(G^{\alpha+\frac12}\,g_{\mu\nu}\,\gamma_{ik}\,\frac{\partial g_{ik}}{\partial x_\nu}\right)$$

$$\gamma_{ik}\,G$$

$$= \sum\frac{\partial}{\partial x_\mu}\left(g_{\mu\nu}\,\gamma_{ik}\,\frac{\partial g_{ik}}{\partial x_\nu}\right) = -\sum\frac{\partial}{\partial x_\mu}\left(g_{\mu\nu}\,g_{ik}\,\frac{\partial \gamma_{ik}}{\partial x_\nu}\right)$$

Anderer Ausdruck für obigen Skalar φ_1

$$_{\mu'}\,g_{\mu\nu}\,\frac{\partial G}{\partial x_\nu}\,g_{\mu'\nu'}\,\frac{\partial G}{\partial x_\mu}$$

Anderer Ausdruck für φ_1

$$\sum\frac{\partial}{\partial x_\mu}\left(G^{\alpha+\frac12}\,g_{\mu\nu}\,\gamma_{ik}\,\frac{\partial g_{ik}}{\partial x_\nu}\right)$$

$$\frac{\partial G}{\partial x_\nu} = -\sum g_{ik}\frac{\partial \gamma_{ik}}{\partial x_\nu}\cdots$$